FRANKIE'S MAGIC FOOTBALL

DEEP SEA DIVE

FRANK LAMPARD

LITTLE, BROWN BOOKS FOR YOUNG READERS
www.lbkids.co.uk

LITTLE, BROWN BOOKS FOR YOUNG READERS

First published in Great Britain in 2016 by Hodder and Stoughton

1 3 5 7 9 10 8 6 4 2

ISBN 978-0-34913-213-6

Typeset in Cantarell by M Rules
Printed and bound in Great Britain by
Clays Ltd, St Ives plc

The paper and board used in this book are made
from wood from responsible sources.

MIX
Paper from
responsible sources
FSC® C104740

Little, Brown Books for Young Readers
An imprint of
Hachette Children's Group
Part of Hodder and Stoughton
Carmelite House
50 Victoria Embankment
London EC4Y 0DZ

An Hachette UK Company
www.hachette.co.uk

www.hachettechildrens.co.uk

*To my mum Pat, who encouraged me
to do my homework in between kicking
a ball all around the house, and is still
with me every step of the way.*

*Welcome to a fantastic
Fantasy League – the greatest
football competition ever held
in this world or any other!*

*You'll need four on a team,
so choose carefully. This is a lot
more serious than a game in the
park. You'll never know who your
next opponents will be, or
where you'll face them.*

*So lace up your boots, players,
and good luck! The whistle's
about to blow!*

The Ref

CHAPTER 1

"Life jackets on, please," said the steward.

Frankie zipped up his bright yellow jacket and looked out across the water. A light drizzle was falling over the holiday camp, so most people had stayed in their cabins, playing board games or watching TV. But Frankie and his friends weren't going to let a little rain spoil their holiday. They'd come to the boating lake with Frankie's brother Kevin. Today, for once, there was no queue. About ten small rowing boats were moored up against the jetty.

Charlie was struggling with his zip. He couldn't grip it properly with his goalie gloves. That was the thing about Charlie – he never took his gloves off. Even in the bath!

"Here, let me help," said Louise. She soon had Charlie's jacket fastened.

Max had already hopped into the nearest boat, his paws resting on the edge.

"Can he swim?" asked the steward, frowning.

"Like a fish," said Frankie.

"All right, then," said the steward. "A few rules. Jackets stay on at *all* times. No standing up in the boats. No splashing with the oars. And no going beyond the buoys." He pointed across the lake to where a line of red inflatables were bobbing in the water.

"Got it," said Frankie.

The steward nodded at the football in Frankie's hand. "Want to leave that with me?"

Frankie clutched the ball tighter. It was falling to bits – the stitching had completely gone down one side. "I'd better keep it with me, thanks."

"OK, you're good to go," said the steward. He watched Frankie and Kevin climb into the boat with Max. The small craft wobbled under Frankie's feet as he settled on the bench. Louise clambered into a second boat, but Charlie remained on the jetty. He chewed his lip nervously.

"What's the matter?" said Kevin. "Don't tell me you're scared of water!"

"I'm not a great swimmer," said Charlie.

"Don't worry," said Louise,

holding out a hand to him. "You've got a life vest on – and anyway, we won't be getting wet."

Charlie stepped into the boat and sat down, smiling weakly.

The steward handed each crew a set of oars. "See you in half an hour," he said, then walked back to his little cabin out of the rain.

Frankie tucked the football under his bench, and saw that Kevin was smirking at him. "Keeping it close, I see," he said.

Frankie ignored him. His brother knew very well what the magic football was capable of, and liked to tease Frankie about it. In fact,

Frankie and his friends would have been enjoying another magical adventure right now if Kevin hadn't tagged along. They'd been planning to go straight to the shut-down theme park on the far side of the camp, but when Kevin had caught up, they'd decided the boating lake was a better idea.

So far, the magic football had brought two rides to life, sending them to a dinosaur world, and into space! They were only here for a few more days, and Frankie was eager to see what rides they could go on next.

Frankie slotted the oars into

place while Kevin unlooped the mooring rope. With a few pulls Frankie propelled them away from the jetty. At first it was hard work and the boat started to drift in the wrong direction.

"You're hopeless!" said Kevin. "Let me have a go."

"Wait," said Frankie. Soon he got the hang of it, and the oars were gliding through the water.

Kevin glanced back towards the steward's cabin, then pulled his life jacket off. "Silly thing," he muttered.

"You shouldn't," said Frankie. "What if you fall in?"

Kevin rolled his eyes. "Don't be such a chicken."

Frankie looked over the side of the boat. The water was too murky to see how deep it was. *Probably not very deep,* he told himself.

Louise pulled up alongside their boat, churning the water. Charlie was gripping the sides, his face a little pale.

"This is fun!" she said. "Harder than it looks, though."

Kevin suddenly reached across and grabbed the oars from Frankie.

"Hey!" said Frankie.

Before he could take them back, Kevin began to slap the paddles

in the water, throwing waves
at Louise's boat. One splashed
Charlie, soaking him.

"That's not funny!" he said.

Frankie sighed. He wished
they'd never brought Kevin with
them.

His brother was laughing as he continued to splash the others, but Louise just sank the oars again, and rowed away.

"Great! Let's race!" said Kevin.

With a lot of rocking, he managed to turn the boat around.

"Maybe we should just go back to shore," said Frankie.

Kevin began to thrash the oars as he tried to row. He wasn't very good, but soon they were veering in an uneven course after Louise. Max whined between Frankie's feet.

Kevin looked back over his shoulder, keeping on track. Frankie saw that Louise had already reached the line of buoys, and she was making a slow, graceful turn.

"Kev, slow down," said Frankie. "We're heading right for them."

His brother grinned. "I know."

He rowed harder, picking up speed.

Charlie saw them coming. "Stop!" he cried.

Frankie stood up to try and grab the oars from his brother, but it was too late.

Louise's boat was side-on when the boats crashed together with a *thump*. Frankie saw it wobble and Charlie wailed as water sloshed over the side. Max barked. Thankfully the boat didn't capsize.

"That was stupid!" Louise cried.

"Just having a bit of a laugh," Kevin said, shrugging his shoulders.

"No one thinks it's funny," Frankie told him.

He noticed that both boats had drifted past the buoys and into water that was thick with weeds. Fallen logs and other debris floated on the surface. Tree branches hung over the water like spindly fingers. Looking beyond to the far bank, Frankie realised they were close to the abandoned theme park. He could see the T. Rex Runaway train ride peeping through the trees.

"Let's get back to the proper lake," he said, taking hold of the oars.

"What's wrong with all of you?" said Kevin sulkily. "Anyone would think you'd never broken a rule before, but I know what you've been up to." He reached with his foot and rolled the football out from under the bench, then stood up. "You've been sneaking into that theme park with this."

He tossed the ball in the air, then started to do keepie-uppies. The boat wobbled from side to side.

"Kev, that's enough!" said Frankie. "Give it back."

"Not until you tell me what's been going on," said Kevin. He kicked the ball high and bent down to try and catch it behind his head. It was a hard enough trick on solid ground and he misjudged it. The ball bounced off the back of his head and splashed into the water a few metres away.

"Nice one!" said Charlie.

Frankie reached out with an oar to scoop up the ball, but saw it wasn't there.

"Where's it gone?" he said, with rising panic.

"Maybe it sank," said Kevin.

"It shouldn't do," said Louise.

The water began to swirl on the surface where the ball had fallen in.

"Uh-oh," said Charlie.

The swirl expanded, spinning quicker and quicker, and in its centre the water dropped as if it was being sucked down a plug-hole. Frankie felt his boat start to drift towards it.

"Quick! Row away!" said Kevin.

Frankie plunged his oars into the water. Louise was doing the same.

But it was no use. The whirlpool grew, and so did its power. It was pulling them in. Max whined and laid a paw across his eyes.

Kevin and Charlie paddled furiously with their hands, scooping up water.

"What's happening?" yelled Kevin, his face twisted with fear.

"It's the magic football!" said Frankie. "Hold on, everyone."

But Kevin must have seen his chance. As the boat's nose dipped into the whirlpool, he jumped clear, grabbing at a branch that was growing over the water. Frankie saw his brother's legs dangling, and then the world lurched over. He tumbled out of the boat.

CHAPTER 2

Frankie took a deep, gasping breath before the water swallowed him. He expected it to be cold, but it wasn't at all. He thrashed in panic, looking for his friends. The bubbles rising all around him meant he couldn't see a thing, so he kicked for the surface.

Suddenly Louise was in front of him, and she was grinning.

"Frankie, stop," she said. "We can breathe underwater!"

And I can hear her voice. That's strange, he thought. Louise's long hair wafted in the gentle, warm currents. Max was bobbing at her side, and Charlie was pulling himself through the water with his gloves. All their life-vests had vanished.

Frankie didn't want to open his mouth — it just felt wrong to let the water rush in.

"Go on, it's fine!" said Max. Scrabbling his paws, he did a backflip in the water.

Well, if it's OK for them . . .

Frankie took a breath and, amazingly, it was just like sucking in air. He felt a smile spread over his lips. His thumping heart began to slow. He gazed around him. Rays of sunlight pierced the clear blue water from above.

"Do you think we're still in the pond?" asked Charlie.

"No way," said Louise. "Feel how warm it is. I think the magic football has brought us to a tropical sea."

"And it must be letting us breathe underwater!" said Frankie. "Speaking of which, where is it?"

"There," said Charlie, pointing.

Frankie looked down and saw the dim shape of the ball, sinking into the depths. "After it!" he cried.

Max's tail whirled like a propeller and his little legs were a blur as he nosed down in pursuit. Frankie and his friends followed. As they swam, Frankie saw a huge shoal of silver fish coming their way. The fish changed course, glinting like coins. He wondered if this was a real ocean, somewhere on Earth, or a magical one. The football could have brought them to either.

He soon saw the football land softly on the sandy seabed. Huge boulders lay strewn across the ocean floor, covered in bristling seaweeds and clinging anemones. A crab scuttled out of sight beneath one.

Frankie picked up the football as the others joined him.

"I wonder why we're here," said Louise. "Normally the football brings us somewhere we can help."

Frankie was about to answer, when he saw a movement to his left. Something streaked from a field of swaying seaweed and disappeared behind a boulder. He couldn't be sure, because it moved so fast, but he thought it might have been another person. Perhaps his brother had fallen into the whirlpool after all ...

"Kevin?" he called.

"I don't think it's Kevin," said Max, twitching his nose. "Doesn't smell like dirty socks."

Frankie swam towards the boulder. "Hello?" he said.

As he got closer, a head poked

out. Frankie jerked back. Max was right – it definitely wasn't Kevin! It was a girl, with lilac skin and green spiky hair. She waved a hand, and Frankie saw that her fingers were webbed. "Hi," she said. "Where are your tails?"

"Our tails?" said Charlie.

"I've got a tail," said Max, wagging his.

"No, like this," said the girl, smiling. She swam up from behind the rock and Frankie gasped. Where her legs should have been was a scaly tail like a fish's.

"You're a mermaid!" said Frankie.

27

"Of course I am," said the girl. "My name is Zoe. But what are you?"

"We're humans," said Louise. She introduced them all, then added, "We normally live on land."

Zoe frowned. "Humans! I thought they were just a legend."

Frankie laughed. "We thought the same about mermaids!"

The mermaid's frown deepened as she looked at Max. "And are you some sort of fur-fish?"

"I'm a dog," said Max.

"A dogfish?"

"No," chuckled Max. "Just a dog."

"Well, you should all come back

to my city," said Zoe. She tipped over with a graceful swish of her tail and swam down again behind the boulder. When she re-emerged she was holding a basket full of what looked like red pears. "I've been collecting sea-fruit for our festival," she said. "Come on!"

As she began to swim away, Frankie shrugged to his friends. "Let's go with her. A festival sounds like fun!"

They all kicked their legs to swim after the mermaid. Even though Frankie was a good swimmer, it was hard to keep up with her.

"Wait for us!" said Charlie.

Zoe slowed and grinned over her shoulder. "I can't wait to show you the city," she said. "It's the most beautiful place in the ocean. My people carved it from a vast coral reef."

As they swam, the sea floor rose up in front of them, towards a ridge. At the top, Zoe suddenly stopped, and the fruit tumbled from her basket. "Oh no!" she cried.

"What is it?" said Frankie, swimming to her side.

Over the ridge he saw the towers of a huge city sprawled

across the ocean floor. There were towers of coral, shaped into arches and domes and pillars, but they seemed to be grey and crumbling. It looked more like a ruin than a thriving city.

"What happened?" asked Louise.

Zoe shook her head. "I don't know. Normally the coral sparkles like a rainbow."

Frankie felt a prickle of unease. Perhaps this was why the football had brought them to the tropical sea.

"Let's go and take a look," he said.

Together, they swam more slowly down into the city. There were fields of limp, dying seaweed covering the seabed, and no fish at all in the water. Complete silence fell over the ruined city.

"Where is everyone?" said Zoe.

At the sound of her voice, a boy with a tail came swimming from under an archway. "Sister!" he cried. "You're back!"

He looked about the same age as Zoe. "Avi! What happened here?" she asked.

"The sharks came," he said sadly. "They took . . ." He stopped as a huge creaking groan filled the water. One of the towers next to the archway began to lean. Right towards them.

"It's going to fall!" cried Frankie.

"Out of the way!" yelled Louise.

As they darted to one side, small bits of coral broke away from the turret and thumped down to the seabed. Then the whole tower collapsed. Avi grabbed Charlie's arm and tugged him along, while Frankie swam alongside Louise and Zoe. He felt the buffeting current caused by the falling tower. It crashed down in a huge cloud of sand where they had been bobbing just a moment before.

"Thanks!" said Charlie. "That was close."

But Frankie realised someone was missing. "Max?" he said.

There was no sign of Frankie's dog.

CHAPTER 3

"Max!" they all shouted, swimming over the debris.

With each second that passed, Frankie's heart sank further. And from the worried looks of the others, he could see they felt the same. *Where are you, boy?*

"I heard something!" said Avi at last.

Then Frankie's ears picked up the sound too — a bark!

"Max?" he called.

More barks. Frankie swam to where the sound was coming from, underneath broken pieces of coral. "Help me dig!" he said to the others.

He seized a chunk of coral, and heaved. It barely budged. Charlie took the other side in his gloves. Together they managed to toss it aside. There was a dark hollow where it had been, then Max stuck his grey snout out. Frankie's heart soared.

"About time!" said Max, paddling

out. He looked completely unharmed, thank goodness. "That was worse than the time I got locked in the neighbour's shed."

Frankie tickled him behind his ears. "Just stay close, boy," he muttered.

"So you were saying, Avi, about the sharks?" said Zoe.

Her brother grimaced. "It was Sammy and his gang. They took the Sea Stone," he said.

Zoe went pale. "Show me."

Frankie wondered what the Sea Stone could be as they followed Zoe and her brother through the ruined city. All the buildings were looking close to collapse, and soon they reached an open square surrounded by crumbling columns. In the centre stood an empty plinth. There were strands of knotted seaweed hanging between the columns, and flags made of different coloured leaves. Frankie guessed they were banners for the festival.

"So much for the celebrations," said Zoe, a silver tear in her eye.

"What is this Stone?" asked Louise.

"It's about as big as that," said Zoe, pointing to the football under Frankie's arm, "but it's shiny like a pearl. The Stone lets us control the seas around the city. We use it to maintain harmony and balance. Without it, the city will disappear into the ocean."

"And some sharks stole it?" said Frankie.

Avi nodded. "The sharks are really greedy and lazy. One called Sammy is in charge. He's always wanted the Stone, because he can use to it control other sea creatures."

"Where is everyone else?" asked Charlie. "Y'know, the merfolk?"

"They went to hide in the Ancient Caves," said Avi. "In case the sharks come back. We should all go there too."

Frankie looked at each of his friends. They stared back with grim determination. It was obvious why the magic football had brought them here.

"First, we'll get the Stone back," he said.

Zoe shook her head. "It's too dangerous. I'm pretty sure the sharks would like the taste of humans ... and dogs."

"I'd like to see them try to eat me," growled Max. "I once took on a lion!"

"You don't have to come," said

Frankie. "Just tell us where to go."

Zoe swallowed. "It's a long way. You have to follow the ravine towards the three peaks." She pointed across the crumbling buildings, to where Frankie could see three underwater mountains. "They live in a house made of metal."

A house made of metal – what's that supposed to mean?

"Well, let's go," said Frankie. He turned to swim away.

"Wait!" said Avi. "It'll take you forever! You'll need a ride."

"A ride?" said Charlie. "On what?"

Avi put his fingers to his mouth, and let out a shrill whistle. A few seconds later, three silver shapes zipped through the water towards them.

"Dolphins!" said Frankie.

"Hop on," said Zoe, as the beautiful creatures drifted alongside them.

Frankie frowned. He'd ridden a horse before on their adventures — how different could this be? He slung a leg over the dolphin's smooth back and gripped its dorsal fin. The others did the same.

"What about me?" asked Max.

Zoe swam down and unfastened

one of the banners. She looped
one end around Max's neck and
fastened the other end to the
dolphin's tail. "There you go," she
said. "Someone can carry you under
their arm, but just to make sure you
don't get separated . . ."

Max didn't look too happy about
wearing a lead, but nodded. "All
right, I suppose."

"OK, we'll come back soon," said
Frankie. "Wish us luck."

Zoe shot a glance at her brother,
who nodded back. "We're coming
with you," she said. "It's our Stone,
we can't just leave it to you."

"Great!" said Frankie.

"So how d'you make it go?" asked Charlie, on his dolphin's back. "Giddy-up, boy!"

The dolphin rolled its eyes. "Actually, you just need to ask politely," the creature told him.

Charlie gasped. "Oh, right. Didn't realise you talked. Er . . . go, please?"

"We're very sensitive and clever creatures," the dolphin explained. "Squeeze lightly with your knees. Steer by pressing lightly with your hands. Maybe take off those gloves."

Charlie looked alarmed and Frankie grinned. He nudged his dolphin's flanks and it shot forward so fast he almost fell off backwards.

Charlie zoomed by at his side. "Woo-hoo!" he cried.

Louise streaked past too, then steered her dolphin upwards, and looped upside down. "This is so much fun!" she called.

It took Frankie a few goes to get used to it, but soon he had the dolphin under control and they were all streaking through the water towards the distant mountains. Zoe and Avi swam at their sides, propelled only by their swishing tails.

After they'd been travelling for

what seemed like ages, the dolphins began to send out high-pitched squeaks.

"What's that?" asked Zoe, cocking her head.

The dolphins sank to the sea floor, chirruping.

"A shark patrol," said Avi. "Up ahead."

Sure enough, through the gloomy water, Frankie saw several dark shapes drifting.

"Can we sneak past?" asked Louise.

Zoe shook her head. "Sharks have amazing noses," she said. "They'd sniff us out quickly."

"What about the tunnels?" asked Avi, nodding towards one of the dark openings. "We could take one of them and get close."

Zoe frowned. "I'm not sure . . . Mum and Dad said we should never go in there alone. We could get lost."

"If it's the only way," said Frankie, "we should take it."

Zoe glanced in the direction of the sharks. "All right, but stay close. We'll leave the dolphins behind."

They slipped off the backs of their animals, and Zoe unfastened Max's lead.

She went first, closely followed

by Frankie. It wasn't quite pitch black inside, because the walls were covered with fluorescent green algae, casting everything in a sickly light. Checking back, he saw his friends' eyes were wide with fear.

The tunnel forked ahead, and Zoe paused, before leading them down the narrower passage. As they reached another junction, Frankie tried to memorise their route for when they needed to come back.

Left ... left ... right – or was it left again?

They entered a tunnel where the bright algae grew only in a few patches. The water here seemed much darker. Colder, too. He could barely see Zoe's tail flashing back and forth in front of him.

"Er ... there's something *moving*," said Louise. "Beneath us."

Frankie looked down. The bottom of the tunnel was shifting. Something snaked from the depths. It grasped for him, but he jerked his leg out of reach. It looked like a tendril, about as wide as his wrist, and covered in suckers.

"Snatcher Weeds!" said Avi. "Swim, everyone!"

More of the temdrils reached up, black and coiling.

They all panicked, flailing in the water. One of the weeds touched Frankie's wrist, cold and slimy, and he batted it away. Then he saw another wrap around Avi's waist. Frankie kicked towards him, and grabbed the tendril. It felt like wrestling an eel, but he managed to prise it off. Avi flicked his tail and

swam upwards. As Frankie kicked
to follow, something fastened like
a vice around his lower leg. He
tugged, but it held him firmly.

"Help me!" he cried, his chest
flooding with panic. "It's got me!"

The plant's strength was
incredible, and Frankie could do
nothing as it dragged him down.

CHAPTER 4

Frankie felt hands grab him. One
of them was wearing a glove. His
friends yanked him up. Frankie felt
the grip of the suckers slip down
his leg and catch on his ankle.
Then he felt his shoe slide off, and
the pressure was gone. He kicked
his legs and let himself be carried
upwards. They all paddled furiously,
until at last Frankie saw the dim

light of a tunnel mouth ahead. It was draped with hanging weeds.

Zoe and Avi were catching their breath at the entrance. Frankie looked down at his leg and saw the tendril had left scratches over his ankle, but otherwise he was unhurt.

"Thanks!" he said to his friends.

"We're almost at the sharks' den," said Zoe. She pushed aside some weeds that hung over the entrance to the tunnel. Beyond, Frankie saw what looked like a submarine lying at an angle on the seabed. Its nose pointed upwards. It had a turret with the hatch hanging open. Dirty portholes lined its side. Lots of them had their glass missing. There were no sharks in sight.

"Sammy lives in there?" said Charlie. "An old shipwreck!"

Zoe nodded.

Frankie had been thinking. "I have a plan," he said. "How about we tempt him out with a distraction, then I'll slip inside and get the Stone?"

Louise frowned. "Sounds dangerous," she said. "If it doesn't work, you'll be trapped."

"We'll *make* it work," said Frankie. "I'll squeeze through one of the portholes," he said, pointing. Looking on the seabed, he saw lots of small rocks. "You guys all take a rock. Throw them at the turret and Sammy will come to see what the noise is."

"OK," said Louise. "But be careful, Frankie."

"Yeah, don't become fish food," added Max.

The others all grabbed a rock each, and they crossed the clearing towards the abandoned submarine. Frankie kept his eyes peeled for sharks. Sammy obviously hadn't expected anyone to sneak in through the tunnels, because there was no patrol here. *Odd*, Frankie thought.

Then he saw a shadow move across the seabed. It was joined by more shadows, flickering darkly. He looked up and his heart jolted. Four shapes, several metres apart, were floating in the water above them. From their paddle-like flippers he realised they were turtles. They were each holding something in their jaws as they swam in a formation. A long, thin line stretched from mouth to mouth, and other strands hung between them. Frankie realised what it was at the same time as Louise.

"A net!" she cried.

The turtles opened their jaws and the trap fell through the water towards them.

Frankie and the others scrambled to get out of the way, but they hadn't had time to form a plan. They banged into each other trying to escape, but it was

too late. The net fell over them.
Frankie tried to kick away, but his
legs were already tangled. Max
scrabbled through one of the
gaps, but the rest of them were
dragged down towards the seabed
in a writhing ball of limbs. As
they bumped into the ocean floor,
Frankie managed to toss the magic
football free.

"Here, Max, take it!" he called.
"Keep it safe."

"I'm not leaving you!" said his
loyal dog.

"Uh-oh – sharks!" said Charlie.

Frankie saw their dark shapes
drift from behind the submarine.

"Go, Max," he said. "Before it's too late!"

Max whined and, taking the football in his jaws, paddled back towards the tunnels. None of the sharks seemed to see him. They all circled the net, watching Frankie and his helpless companions. Frankie had seen a shark in an aquarium before, but then he'd been safe behind a pane of thick glass. This was very different. Their sleek, muscular bodies and unblinking eyes made his skin crawl.

"We're not scared of you!" said Zoe, with a tremble in her voice.

Then one of the sharks broke

away from the others and darted towards them, gripping the net in its teeth. With a flick of its tail, it dragged them towards the submarine. Pressed up close to his friends, Frankie bumped into the side of the rusty hatch as they were pulled inside. The hatch slammed shut behind them with a dull *clang.* A light was shining along a central corridor.

"Sammy must be using the Stone to enslave the turtles," whispered Zoe.

The shark pulled them along, through another hatch, and into a large chamber. The portholes were all covered in grime, but it was clear where the light was coming from. Sitting in an open clamshell the size of a fruit bowl was a pearl almost twenty centimetres across. It glowed like a white bulb, and its surface shimmered with rainbow colours.

"The Sea Stone!" said Zoe.

"Pretty, isn't it?" said a gravelly voice.

They all twisted round in the net to see a huge, fat shark swimming from the shadows. It brushed the pearl with its tail fin, then rounded on them.

"And it's all mine!" the creature added.

"It belongs to the merfolk, Sammy," said Frankie.

"Not any more," said Sammy. "I can't believe you fell right into my trap. That was too easy!"

"What shall we do with them, boss?" said the shark who'd dragged them inside.

"Put them in the hold for now," said Sammy. "Olly the octopus is giving me my three o'clock massage, then I'll need a nap. That should work up a nice," he glanced at them, "*appetite*."

Frankie gulped. *I don't like the sound of that.*

CHAPTER 5

The sharks put them in a small
chamber of the submarine. Still
tangled in the net, Frankie was
stuck upside down. There wasn't
even enough space to swing
himself upright.

"Maybe they won't like the
taste of humans," said Charlie
hopefully.

"And how are they going to find

that out," asked Louise, "unless they taste *one of us* first?"

"We're not going to get eaten," said Frankie. He grabbed two strands of the net and tried to pull them apart. If he could just make a gap big enough, perhaps they could slip free. After gritting his teeth and tugging for several seconds, he felt the ropes cutting into his hands and gave up. "It's no use!" he said. "We're stuck."

"Sorry we got you into this mess," said Zoe. "This isn't even your problem."

For a long time, they simply hung in the water. Avi's scaly tail was draped over Louise's head, and Charlie's foot was digging into Frankie's back, but it was pointless complaining. They were all in the same boat – well, submarine.

"Never fear, Max is here!" barked a voice.

"Shh!" said Louise.

Frankie saw his dog's wagging tail sticking in from a porthole. He squeezed through backwards, bottom first. As his head popped in as well, Frankie saw Max had the magic football in his jaws.

"Sorry it's taken me a while," said Max. "Sharks everywhere."

"Hey, boy!" Frankie said. "Any

chance you can chew through this net?"

"If I can chew through your dad's leather belt, a bit of old rope shouldn't cause any problems."

Max got to work gnawing at the net, thrashing his head from side to side. Frankie kept looking towards the hatch, expecting a shark to burst in. The strand of the net frayed, and thinned, and finally broke. The gap was only about thirty centimetres wide, but Frankie managed to wriggle through. He untied the ends of the net, and released the others.

"You saved our lives, dogfish,"
said Zoe, stroking his head.

Frankie knew Max was blushing
under his fur.

Avi was already at the porthole.
"We should be able to squeeze out
this way," he said.

Charlie and Louise joined him,
but Frankie hung back. There was
unfinished business to deal with.

"Come on, let's go!" said Zoe.

"What about the Sea Stone?"
asked Frankie.

"Just leave it," said Zoe. "Only
catfish have nine lives. We're lucky
we're not a shark buffet right
now."

Frankie looked at their defeated faces. It reminded him of a game a few months before, when they'd been three-nil down at half-time to Holly Road Primary. In the dressing room, everyone had looked ready to pack it in. But he remembered his football coach's words.

"It's not over until the final whistle," Frankie said.

Zoe's brow furrowed. "What whistle?"

Louise moved away from the porthole, her eyes shining. "Frankie's right. We can do this."

Charlie joined them. "We stick together. Play as a team."

Avi smiled weakly, but Zoe's jaw tightened. "Let's do it."

With Frankie going first, they swam to the hatch that opened back into the main chamber of the submarine. Frankie peered through the crack. It was dark on the other side, and he saw the clamshell was closed. *The Stone must be inside still,* he thought. In the dim light, he saw Sammy was on his back, floating in the water. His eyes were closed – he was taking a nap.

Frankie beckoned for Charlie and Louise to swim for the main hatch, and slipped out into the chamber. He swam towards the clam shell with Max at his heels. Sammy didn't stir. He took hold of the edges of the clamshell and eased them open. The glowing pearl cast its light across the chamber. Frankie swallowed, expecting the shark's eyes to open, but Sammy didn't move. Frankie gently lifted the Stone in both hands as Max bobbed beside him. It felt smooth, and warm, and surprisingly light. He was removing it from the shell when someone tapped him on the shoulder.

"Excuse me," said a voice he didn't recognise. "Where d'you think you're going with that?"

Frankie spun around, and found himself face to face with a huge, bulbous octopus, floating in the water. Sammy grunted in his sleep.

The octopus grabbed Frankie's arms in its tentacles. "Intruders!" it screamed.

Frankie dropped the pearl, and kicked it between the octopus's

several legs. Max caught it on his nose and began to swim towards the hatch as Sammy rolled upright. "What's going on?" he yawned.

Frankie thrashed to free his arms from the octopus, and managed to get one loose. He prised the second tentacle off his other arm. Before the octopus could wrestle free, Frankie quickly tied its tentacles in a knot.

Sammy's eyes widened. "The Stone! They're getting away with it!"

The shark surged across the chamber, to where Max was slipping through the main submarine hatch. Louise must have been waiting outside, because the hatch door slammed closed just as the shark reached it. He thumped into the metal door, nose-first, with a roar of pain.

With the octopus still tangled, Frankie quickly swam back to the hold where they'd been imprisoned. He scrambled through the porthole and into open water. The others were waiting and Charlie had the magic football tucked under his arm. Sharks were closing in all around. Max was last to escape, still pushing the Stone with his snout.

Suddenly a crab scuttled out of a porthole and clamped its pincers on Max's tail.

Frankie's dog yowled in pain and let the Stone bounce off the submarine's hull towards the seabed. Louise dived after it, but a turtle was coming the other way. It buffeted her aside like a defender barging her off the ball. Frankie went down to retrieve the pearl. He just had it in his hands when the octopus squeezed through a porthole beside him.

It screeched at him, jetting out black ink into the water.

Frankie couldn't see a thing as

the dark cloud enveloped him, but he felt the Stone torn from his grasp. He pushed off the sea floor, trying to get clear. As he did, he saw Louise and Max and Charlie. *Oh no!* They were surrounded by sharks. Avi and Zoe must have managed to get away to the tunnels, because he couldn't see them anywhere.

Sammy eased his bulk through the submarine's hatch. His face was twisted with anger.

Frankie thought back to the first time Avi had summoned the dolphins. *I hope they're listening now*, he thought. He put his fingers in his mouth and whistled loudly.

Frankie looked out past the sharks. *Yes! There they were!* Grey shapes were speeding through the water – the dolphins. "Get ready," he muttered to his friends.

"Attack!" Sammy ordered the sharks.

The sharks shot forward as one, eyes rolling back in their heads. But they weren't quick enough. The dolphins parted and swam around them, swooping past. Frankie quickly scooped up Max under his arm, then reached out and gripped a dorsal fin. His friends grabbed on to their own dolphins. They were off! He only just managed to hang on as they surged away, out of reach of the snapping sharks.

"After them!" cried Sammy.

The dolphins carried them towards the tunnel entrance, where Avi and Zoe were waiting. "Quickly! They're gaining," called Zoe.

Frankie didn't dare look back. He squeezed his dolphin's flanks hard, and leant close over its back as they cut through the water. Louise disappeared inside first, then Charlie. Frankie's dolphin went after them. Letting go of Max, he toppled off its back and thumped into the tunnel wall.

What now?

A second later the whole tunnel shook as Sammy's head burst in. But the massive shark was wedged in the tunnel entrance. He grimaced and shook, but he couldn't get through.

"Ha!" said Avi. "That's what you get for being so greedy."

The shark scowled at them. "You haven't got the Stone, though! Your city's still finished."

Frankie realised he was right. The magical pearl was stuck on the other side, and now there was no way to get it back. He turned to the others. "I'm sorry. I've let you down."

"Never mind," said Zoe. "You did your best."

They all left Sammy snarling in the tunnel entrance and made their way back towards the ravine. This time, the dolphins led them a different way to avoid the deadly Snatcher Weeds. By the time they emerged into the open ocean again, Frankie was feeling really bad. And not just for the merfolk. He'd never failed on an adventure before.

"What if the magic football doesn't let us go on more adventures?" he said to Louise.

She sighed. "It's looking pretty battered anyway," she replied.

Frankie looked over at the ball, held by Charlie. His friend had a glint in his eye and a smile on his lips.

"Why are you looking so cheerful?" asked Max.

"Because," said Charlie, "I've been keeping a little secret."

He held out the football, and Frankie noticed a tiny glow coming from one of the seams.

CHAPTER 6

Frankie remembered how the pearl had been taken from his grasp in the ink-cloud. He'd thought it was the octopus ...

Charlie peeled back the leather to reveal the Sea Stone.

"I grabbed it in the confusion," said Charlie, when everyone had finished patting him on the back. "I didn't want to say anything sooner in case the sharks heard."

Frankie grinned. His friend had saved the day, and saved the ocean!

They all sped back to the city, with the Sea Stone still hidden inside the beat-up football. But when they arrived, Zoe's home looked worse than before. Almost none of the towers remained and a fine layer of sand was scattering across the ruins. There were people here now, though, carrying sacks of possessions over their shoulders. A merwoman glanced over at them and her hands flew to her face.

"Avi! Zoe!" she cried. "You're alive."

She sped over and swept them up in her arms. A merman quickly joined her. "We thought the sharks had got you!" he said, wiping away a silver tear.

"Frankie, these are our parents," said Zoe. "Mum, Dad, this is Frankie and his friends. They have a surprise!"

Frankie stretched the football's leather seam and pushed out the Sea Stone. Its gleam lit up the ocean.

"It can't be!" said Zoe's mother.

As the light from the pearl

spread across the city, the other
merfolk swam over. Raised voices
spread through the ruins. Frankie
carried the Sea Stone towards the
plinth where it belonged. As he
lifted it up, everyone cheered. It
was almost as if he was holding
the World Cup!

He placed the pearl gently in

its resting place. It glowed more brightly than ever, lighting up the ocean with rays of red and gold. The seas suddenly came alive with hundreds of fish and the banners flickered in the current, shining. He saw now why the Sea Stone was so special.

"I think this calls for the festival to begin!" said Zoe's father. "Better late than never!"

Among the gathered merfolk, several took out musical instruments made of sparkling shells. They started to play. Zoe grabbed Frankie's arm and whirled him round, while Avi pulled Max and Louise into a conga line around the plinth.

"I don't know the steps!" cried Charlie, as Zoe's mother took him by the hands.

"There aren't any," Zoe called back. "We don't have feet, remember!"

Soon everyone was joining in, dancing across the square in time with the music. The city was still in ruins, but Frankie knew it wouldn't be long before the magic of the Stone rebuilt it again. In fact, already new buds of coral were sprouting up in the cracks, spreading colour through the rubble.

Something snagged at Frankie's waist and he saw it was Max, tugging at his T-shirt. "Hate to break up the party," he said, "but the football's doing something." He pointed with his paw. "Over there."

Frankie looked at the football. It was rolling gently across the sea floor to the edge of the square, its seams sparkling silver.

"We have to go," he said to Zoe. "Thanks for a fun adventure!"

"I'm not sure I'd call it fun," she replied. "Where are you heading now?"

"Back home," replied Frankie. The football was beginning to spin in the water, and around it he could see a whirlpool forming, like an underwater tornado.

Frankie led the others towards it. The music still played, but the merfolk had stopped dancing to watch. The football was a swirl as it spun round and round.

"Ready?" said Frankie, reaching out a hand to Louise. She took it, and Charlie took hers. Frankie nodded to Zoe and her brother and they waved back. Then Frankie tucked Max under his arm, and moved into the spinning current. It snatched him up, and everything became a blur.

The water was suddenly freezing cold, and Frankie's chest tightened. He felt his feet sinking into squelchy mud, and his head broke the surface.

He gasped as air rushed into his lungs.

He was standing in the shallows of the boating lake, back at the holiday camp. Louise was right at his side, shivering in sodden clothes. Charlie had a bit of brown weed draped over his head, while Max was splashing to the bank with a furious doggy paddle. The two boats were both upside-down.

Frankie heard someone yelling.

"Help! Help me! I don't have a life-jacket."

Kevin.

Turning around in the water, Frankie saw his brother hanging from a branch. With a cry of panic, he let go and splashed into the water. Frankie waded over to him. His brother was flailing wildly, spluttering.

"It's all right," said Frankie, helping him stand. "It's only about a metre deep."

Kevin went bright red, but he looked relieved as his feet touched the bottom. "Yeah, I knew that," he said. "I was just messing around."

"You looked pretty scared to me," said Charlie, smirking.

Kevin scowled, but then leapt back as an orange lifebelt attached to a rope slammed into the water beside them. The steward stood on the bank, holding the other end. "What happened?" he called. "Why aren't you wearing your life-jacket?"

"There was a whirlpool!" said Kevin. "It tipped us out."

The steward shook his head. "Really? A whirlpool? Any sea monsters? Lost shipwrecks?"

"I'm telling the truth!" shouted Kevin, dragging himself to the bank. "It's the magic football that did it." Frankie should have known his brother would never be able to keep the football's secret.

Luckily, the steward rolled his eyes. "Sure, of course it is. Why didn't I guess? Talking of football, I think you should all stick to playing on dry land from now on. Boating obviously isn't for you."

Frankie scrambled onto the bank, then reached back to help Louise up too. Despite being soaked through, she was grinning.

"I think that might be good advice," she said, turning to the steward. "After all, what trouble can we get into with a football?"

As she spoke, Frankie hid his magic football behind his back. There were still sparkles of silver escaping from the seams. Kevin stalked away angrily and the friends laughed as they watched his soggy footprints disappear across the holiday camp.

"I hope Sammy can forgive us for stealing the Sea Stone away from him," Charlie said, clapping his sodden gloves together to squeeze the water out.

Frankie slapped a hand on his friend's shoulder. "That wasn't stealing, that was liberating," he said. He'd never forget the feeling of lifting the Sea Stone onto the plinth. *Maybe I will hold the World Cup,* he thought, as they made their way back. *One day . . .*

ACKNOWLEDGEMENTS

Many thanks to everyone at Hachette Children's Group; Neil Blair, Zoe King, Daniel Teweles and all at The Blair Partnership; Luella Wright for bringing my characters to life; special thanks to Michael Ford for all his wisdom and patience; and to Steve Kutner for being a great friend and for all his help and guidance, not just with the book but with everything.

Competition Time

COULD YOU BE A WINNER LIKE FRANKIE?

Every month one lucky fan will win an exclusive
Frankie's Magic Football goodie bag! Here's how to enter:

Every **Frankie's Magic Football** book
features different animals. Go to:
www.frankiesmagicfootball.co.uk/competitions
and name three different animals that feature in three
different **Frankie's Magic Football** books.
Then you could be a winner!

You can also send your entry by post by filling in
the form on the opposite page.

Once complete, please send your entries to:

Frankie's Magic Football Competition
Hachette Children's Books, Carmelite House,
50 Victoria Embankment,
London, EC4Y 0DZ

GOOD LUCK!

Competition Entry Page

Please enter your details below:

1. Name of Frankie Book: ....
   Animal: ....

2. Name of Frankie Book: ....
   Animal: ....

3. Name of Frankie Book: ....
   Animal: ....

My name is: ....

My date of birth is: ....

Email address: ....

Address 1: ....

Address 2: ....

Address 3: ....

County: ....

Post Code: ....

....

Parent/Guardian signature: ....

FRANKIE'S MAGIC FOOTBALL WEBSITE

Have you had a chance to check out **frankiesmagicfootball.co.uk** yet?

Get involved in **competitions**, find out **news** and **updates** about the series, play **games** and watch **videos** featuring the author, **Frank Lampard!**

Visit the site to join **Frankie's FC** today!